20,000 LEAGUES UNDER THE SEA

20,000 LEAGUES UNDER THE SEA

By Jules Verne

Adapted by Lillian Nordlicht
Illustrated by Steve Butz

RSVP
RAINTREE
STECK-VAUGHN
P U B L I S H E R S
The Steck-Vaughn Company

Austin, Texas

Library of Congress Number: 79-23887

Library of Congress Cataloging-in-Publication Data

Nordlicht, Lillian.
  20,000 leagues under the sea.

  SUMMARY: An adaptation of the 19th-century science fiction tale of an electric submarine, its eccentric captain, and undersea world which anticipated many of the scientific achievements of the 20th century.
  [1. Sea stories. 2. Submarines—Fiction.
3. Science fiction] I. Butz, Steve. II. Verne, Jules, 1828-1905. Vingt mille lieues sous les mers. III. Title.
PZ7.N77547Tw   [Fic.]   79-23887

ISBN 0-8172-1652-9 hardcover library binding

ISBN 0-8114-6846-1 softcover binding

18 19 20   99 98